THE LAST ONE:
JFK RETURNS

Mary F. Carruthers

Copyright © 2018

Mary F. Carruthers

ISBN-13: 9781980584636

DEDICATION

To my best friend and husband,
Michael.   My love and gratitude for
all you've done for me in my life

Acknowledgements:

I give thanks to Jesus Christ Who gave me the courage to become a writer and to give free rein to my imagination.

TABLE OF CONTENTS

ACKNOWLEDGMENTS

I give thanks to God Who gave me
the courage to become a writer, and to
give free rein to my imagination.

CHAPTER one

Up in the top floors of a skyscraper, nestled in the scraper complexes of New York City, a lone man sat and leaned back, looking out at the panoramic view of NY's Central Park below. His mien looked vaguely familiar. He looked like anyone really, much like a well-heeled businessman, successful in the way he dressed. His face was tanned, his eyes were blue, and his features were what some people might call "All-American".

His figure was hale and fit, as though he played football in college. He looked about 35 years old. His eyes, clear and direct, became clouded as his mind flew back to 1963. He saw adoring crowds as he sat in an open limousine which made its way through the streets of Dallas. His wife was beside him. She was clad in pink. Pink pillbox hat, pink suit, and gloves that she wore as she waved happily. Her smile was wide. She looked beautiful. He recalled how happy and unaware they were of what was about to happen that day. His memory stopped there. There was no trace of his violent death now. At all. His back was straight with no memory of injuries sustained in World War II. But this day, a clear day which had no clouds in the sky, John Fitzgerald Kennedy was a normal human being for all intents and purposes. He felt no anxieties, nor did he have any second thoughts at all of why he had returned back from Heaven. No second thoughts from the information that he was given some time ago.

JFK's gaze ran over the copse of trees on the edge of Central Park West. His thoughts ran back to when he stood facing a benign older man. He called himself Mr. Mercer. Mercer seemed without peer in Intelligence, and did not look like anyone in particular, nor did he have the type of appearance that showed age. Yet his eyes were wise beyond telling and his smile faint, but kind. Mercer was his "Operator".

"John – may I call you John?"

"Yes, although back on earth they called me Jack."

"I don't wish to call you Jack, due to the formalities of your having been christened John." Mr. Mercer said coolly. He tilted his head as he glanced at him. "However, you may tell others to call you Jack." Mercer paused then asked, "Are you anxious to go back to your earthly life?"

"Yes, Mr. Mercer. I am."

"Do you agree to what we have proposed to you?"

"Yes. I agree. I will be looking for who it is that ordered my death. That Last One."

"Good. You know, John, that you won't ever die. We have gone over that before. Think of yourself as having a heavenly body, that cannot suffer injuries nor the aches and pains of ordinary living. So, it means that you can't be killed again, not by anyone. This is what you must keep in mind."

"Yes. That is what gives me the confidence that this assignment is going to succeed."

Mr. Mercer turned away a slight angle as another man appeared at his side.

"This is Michael." The man named Michael looked at John Kennedy and gave him a slight nod. Michael was clad in a modern suit, gray with an open neck shirt. He looked like a successful businessman – someone who mixed with the higher levels of society.

Mr. Mercer continued: "Michael's full name for this mission is Michael Hanes. His team is called F5. They - his men and women - are now deployed on earth. You won't know who they are. They are there as your support and team mates. Michael will be your contact."

Michael said, "John, you and I will be seeing each other in New York City. You'll live in an anonymous address off of Central Park West. You and I will be doing business together – you are an emerging writer and I will be your manager. My job on earth will

be as an entertainment czar who
mixes with the high and glamorous
world of publishing and cinema."
"They won't really know it's me, will
they? Despite the fact that I've not
changed my appearance since 1963?"
"No. Human beings will be
prevented from recognizing you."
Mr. Mercer interjected.
Mercer gave a small cough before
saying, "I have to confess we did that
once before and it was amusing when
it happened. However, it was a way
to camouflage Someone's real identity
– and it is either a permanent thing or
temporary. The citizens of Heaven
are blessed that way." He continued,

"Now, let's see how it goes, shall we? I am sure you will find all you need in your new lodgings." He turned to Michael, and said to him, "Michael, I want to talk to you about Atlas who will be delivering the coup de grace." JFK looked up with a gleam in his eye. "I'd like to kill that sonofabitch if I may."

Michael and Mr. Mercer exchanged a look. Michael said, "No, John. I think you must let our Team handle this. It will be more expeditious."

"Ok, I suppose I'll have to thank Atlas when he has performed his duty."

"John, your job is to be like everyone else. Travel if you like. Meet people.

You will be lionized. There will be a lot of people who will want to invite you to their parties and shows and whatever it is that these awful people do nowadays."

"I am to be lionized." Echoed JFK thoughtfully.

"You will get the publicity that authors with something to say will receive. Perhaps John, you will meet famous celebrities who will have powerful connections."

"Ah, so I will become a curiosity?"

"Yes. You will be the snare we will use to lure the Last One, John." Mercer said with a laugh. Then his face became solemn. "We want that

Last One, John Fitzgerald Kennedy. I am thinking this is something of a cat and mouse game. And you will be the mouse."

CHAPTER two

November 22, 1963: Dallas morgue.

The atmosphere outside the small
room in the morgue was somber, and
yet fraught with tension. The people
who were close to the President were
clustered in one of the offices and the
pathologist gave a short update on the

state of the President's injuries. The pathologist intoned that the President would not have survived that one bullet that hit his skull and exploded inside his brain. There was a hushed silence and everyone's attention shifted to President Kennedy's wife Jackie. She looked as though she had been shot as well, with blood stains on her pink suit and even on her pink pillbox hat. Her gloves were dark with blood. She looked almost as though she was in a catatonic state. Her face was pale, and her lips were slightly trembling. Someone decided to take her out to a private room to mourn, and then she suddenly asked to see her husband one last time before they gave him the preparations for his funeral.

In the room his body lay on a gurney, wrapped only in a sheet. Jackie approached and stood very close to his side. She didn't feel able to take his appearance. It seemed an eternity before she could touch his shoulder, and then she finally spoke softly - so softly that nobody who might have been there could have heard. Then she planted a soft kiss on his pale lips and stepped away. She stood by the door for a moment before straightening herself and opening the door to pass through. The noise outside jarred her tender sensibilities and then someone she knew took her away and drove her back to the waiting Air Force One.

Back in the room where JFK lay, there was a strange light that came from within the room. There was a murmur of voices - disembodied, and then a moment later, a tall and bright figure stepped forward to look at JFK's dead body. The bright figure was clad in a robe of gold brocade, with sunlight glinting from its intricate designs. His face was brightly lit from within and he had piercing blue eyes and his head was wreathed in white curly hair. He looked over his shoulder and made a motion to someone unseen. A short moment after, a silent exchange happened. Within a second, the body of JFK was lifted out until it became unseen, leaving an inert figure that remained shrouded on the gurney. Right after, the bright figure was gone.

CHAPTER three

The meeting among the Angels was delayed since Michael, their leader, has been in communications with God. The angels that were gathered in the hallowed halls of Valhalla - or Heaven, to the ordinary bystander - numbered six. They were all almost alike in mien, almost all had haloes on their fair heads, and they all were clothed in medieval garb. Their uniforms weren't really too different among them. All wore tall leather boots that were tanned and soft to the touch. Their capes were all like the one that took JFK's body away - gold, intricately designed, sparkling with each slight movement. They had a simple tunic each, mostly made of a light green linen. None of them wore any jewelry. They all had swords hanging at their sides. They took sips of an ambrosia like substance from ornate goblets while murmuring with each other in a language that wasn't discernible or understandable.

The oaken door of the hall opened suddenly, and the angels turned to face the One, Michael, who entered. His handsome face was as brightly hued as before and his smile was humorous as he surveyed his angel team. "Everyone ready?"

One of them, whose name was Loreto, said: "I am. But we're all at sea why we have to be in different locations."

The next one was Helena, who looked at her other siblings and said, "I am too. I prefer that we all stayed with the President."

"No need." Michael said shortly. "I've been with the President and we have agreed I will keep an eye on him as he lives out his mission in New York City. I do think there will be one of you, Lohar," He nodded at the angel who was across him who looked on with interest. "You will have a place in the Law office of Graham and Peel. You will be someone that can check on the President on occasion."

"We are ready." They all spoke in unison.

"I'll be on the West coast," Volunteered Roswald, the one who stood closest to Michael.

"I'll be in the Midwest," spoke Adelbert, who looked slightly unconcerned. "Just give me a chime as usual. We are sure that the Last One isn't there." He gave a laugh.

Michael's face did not register any reaction. "Yes, but we have some idea that the Last One has connections there."

"We'll all be in telepathic mode as always on earth. We are all positioned to be in the USA. We won't have to divulge where we really are, but I will ask everyone to check in with me morning and evening. And if there's any developments, you may always clue me in."

"The President is ready, then?"

Michael said, "Yes."

"We are concerned about the fact that his wife is still in heaven and wants to join him." Helena said.

"No, not right now." Michael said
with a serious face. "She isn't ready."

A small sound by the door made them
all turn around. A tall figure, with
ruddy cheeks and wavy red hair
looked in and smiled cheerfully.

"Atlas, you came finally." Michael's
face registered a hint of excitement.

"I've been practicing." Atlas said in a
ringing voice. "I want to be the one.
The one to deliver the mortal blow."

"We are with you there." Echoed the
others. They all gave a cheer.

With that, they dispersed and
everyone, disappeared.

CHAPTER four

The Landing

The F5 Team have landed. Each has
been given their assigned
designations and have blended into
the communities in the cities of New
York, Dallas, Chicago, Santa Barbara,
Beverly Hills, and San Francisco.

Adelbert was received into a Benedictine monastery close to the outskirts of Chicago.

Helena was accepted into UC Santa Barbara as a student majoring in English Literature.

Lohar became law clerk working in Justice Mendel's court (Mendel is in the US Court of Appeals) in New York City.

Loreto was hired as press secretary for the governor of Texas at his Dallas headquarters.

Roswald has taken residence in Beverly Hills working for a greenhouse as a summer worker. Michael, Team Leader, has residences in both San Francisco and New York City. His job on earth is in the field of entertainment.

CHAPTER five

Helena

The halls of UC Santa Barbara School
of Liberal Arts are wide and yet
darkened with the color of old
mahogany walls. Outside the college
of Fine Arts, the day is bright, as it

always seems to be in that part of the world. The students are having a mid-morning break, having gone to classes earlier and then forming separate groups on the front lawn, reading, conversing, checking email on their cell phones and eating snacks that they have bought from the food trucks serving tacos and wraps. There are stairs leading up to the building, which they call "Mandel Building" and on the stairs stood a lone figure of a woman who studying her course syllabus in *Intro to Shakespeare*. She is simply clad in jeans and t-shirt with a cardigan sweater. Her book bag is a nondescript one, probably taken from a thrift shop, and her small purse dangles from her wrist. She looks out at the scene before her. "All set." She says in her mind.

"Good."

"I'm just blending in. I'll check in later."

"I'll be with you then."

Someone passed by and took a look at her. "You look lost. Can I help you?"

She looked at the person and saw a middle-aged professor-type. "No, I'm fine."

"You look new." He persisted.

"Yes, I am. I'm a freshman."

"Did you go through the Freshman Initiation?" He was the friendly California type, she decided.

"Yes, I am heading for that now."

"Good. I don't want to make students feel lost. This is a big campus. My name is Oliver Steele, professor of English Literature. You'll probably have me for your professor in a few years. Maybe earlier." He said with alacrity. "What is your name?"

"Lena Muldoon." She said offering her hand. He shook it. She didn't care for the slight pressure his hand gave hers.

"Muldoon. Sounds English."

"I'm a quarter English and three quarters Irish."

Professor Steele looked enigmatically at her. "Oh. I see. Well, see you around." He waved her off and left.

She looked after him and then shook her head. *"What a creep."* She thought.

"He isn't good, Helena. Stay away from him." The answering thought came to her mind.

"No. I won't want to meet him again."

"Wait, I'm getting the idea that he's in with the publishing crowd there."

"Are you sure?"

"Yes. I'd keep an open mind about him. But keep your distance."

She walked towards the sidewalk and almost bumped into a tall figure who was carrying a basketball. "Oops, sorry!" Lena said.

"I am sorry, I hope I didn't get you." The tall figure stooped down. He had a wide smile and looked quite youthful. His face was marked with a lot of spots. "You new here?"

"Yes, I am."

"I'm Ryan Greene. I am a basketball player - just got accepted."

"Hi Ryan. I'm Lena Muldoon."

"Hey, maybe you and I can get together, and you can watch me play?" He said earnestly.

Lena smiled coolly. "I'm sorry, my boyfriend won't like that. But you can get us tickets and we can watch you."

His smile faded. "Ok. Good to meet ya. See ya around." He bounced his basketball sadly as he walked away.

CHAPTER six

Adelred

Matins was almost over. The monks
had gathered in the large stain-glass
chapel intoning prayers in a deep sing
song. A tall monk came in hurriedly
and took his place at the last pew.
The sound of his arrival, while silent

enough, made some heads turn. One of the others, an elderly monk with a bristly grey beard, looked keenly at the newcomer. The newcomer was a man of middle years, yet he had the stature of someone who had not been fatigued by life nor by time. The grey bearded monk caught the new monk's eye and they gave each other a cordial nod. The grey bearded monk looked back towards the front of the chapel and joined the chorus of the Closing Prayer.

Adelred stood still as he perceived a thought descending upon his consciousness. "That man you don't want to talk to too much, Adelred."

"Agreed." Adelred replied in his thoughts. In the corner of his eye, he sensed the grey bearded monk stir slightly.

Adelred thought of nothing else although he communicated that the grey bearded monk was dangerous.

CHAPTER seven

Lohar

Lohar took a quick glance at his wristwatch as he made the move to cross the street at 65 and Lexington. "Watch out!" Someone yelled at him. He glanced up and saw the oncoming bus. He jumped back into the sidewalk. "You ok?" The person who called after him asked. Lohar beheld a short stocky man with glasses, and a beer belly. "You really almost got creamed there, guy!"

"Yeah. Thanks a bunch! I'm much obliged." Lohar smiled at him.

"You aren't from around here, I can tell already." Grinned the stocky man. "I'm not going to be around all the time to keep you out of trouble, Mister, so you better keep your wits about you, ok?" He reached out a hand and shook Lohar's.

Lohar smiled at him and felt a twinge of unhappiness.

"Don't worry, Lohar. It's a common thing with the new recruits." The thought came to his frazzled mind.

"I hate having to be told someone human is needing to watch over me." Lohar replied silently. He finally crossed the street and entered the building directly ahead of him. The office of Justice Mandel was housed in this building, and it also housed about another hundred offices, some that were law offices and some retail and business. He hopped onto the elevator just as it was about to close and then stood quietly with a crowd of workers, watching the numbers of the floors lit above them. He took his floor and walked towards the eastern hallway and found his new office. A pleasant faced woman

wearing dark rimmed glasses and an animal print blouse and dark slim skirt looked up at him. Her smile widened when she saw how handsome he looked. "Hello, may I help you?" She asked, knowing his name already. She knew everyone who was going and coming in Mandel's offices. "I'm Lola Krebs."
"Mr. Lohar, here to start my new job." Lohar smiled at her.
"Sure! Nice to meet you, Mr. Lohar. Er-" She looked up at him with a twinkle. "Do you have a first name?"
"Er- Adam." Said Lohar.
"Careful, she's really a witch." The thought came to him.

"Adam, pleased to meet you. Let me take you to Justice Mandel's Admin. His name is Myron. Myron Biggs."
"I was hoping I'd meet Justice Mandel himself."
"Oh, no. Mandel's too busy. He will meet all his new staff later on. They'll send an invite. Don't be shocked by the lack of social graces, Adam. It's New York. It's like that here."
"Oh, ok."
"Where are you from originally?"
Adam looked innocently at her. "I'm from Ohio. Columbus."
"Oh." Her face fell in disappointment. "Ok, let's get you

into your office, shall we?" She
turned on her heel and led him down
the office corridor.

CHAPTER eight

Roswald

The landscape of Beverly Hills California is one of lush wealth, exuding all kinds of flora and some unique fauna. Roswald drove his rented Corolla down on Crimson Street where his greenhouse manager told him to go. His assignment was to cut the grass - about a five-acre swath in the exclusive neighborhood of Greenhills. The rickety Corolla

heaved to at the large iron gate. A disembodied voice spoke from the speaker at the gate post. "Who is that calling?"
"Randy Roswald, from Hastings Greenhouse. I've been told to come and cut your grass."
"Ok. I'll put you through. Mrs. Danforth is going to show you to the shed."

The gates opened as if by magic and Roswald drove his heaving Corolla through. He looked at the beautiful mansion in front of him - a work of art and architecture. A red tile roof reminiscent of the Spanish-style, and the gleaming stone walls that shone pale peach in the sun. Several rows of bushes, with brilliant flowers of hibiscus and bougainvillea waved gently in the breeze. On the front porch there stood a large statue of an Oriental soldier as though to herald guardians that weren't really there. Roswald raised his eyebrow and then focused on the woman who was coming out of the black oak door.

"Mr. Roswald?" She seemed nice enough to extend her slim hand. Roswald guessed she wasn't the owner. They never came to talk to the hired help.

"Yes. Call me Randy."

"Randy, then." Her face was tanned and her hand was rough to the touch. "I'm Mrs. Danforth. I'm the housekeeper. The owner of the house, Mrs. Atwell, has sacked the gardener and now we need somebody to at least cut the lawn."

"Sorry to hear that." Roswald said politely.

"Here let me take you to the shed. The riding mower is inside. I will give you the key and then you just have to ring the doorbell and I'll come out and take it from you once you're done."

"Good enough." Roswald nodded and followed her to the far side of the house.

The "shed" was a huge edifice, equaling the house in grandness. This was not a regular shed where one kept the lawnmower and tools for the garden. It was also stucco, and there was a massive double door that had twin X's on each door that were made of brass. A shield of armor decorated the apex of the doors, and on it was a coat of arms. Roswald recognized it as that of the Reynolds family crest. A throwback to someone noble in England, he surmised. Or that the family tried to connect themselves to

someone noble and probably
notorious in England. Roswald rolled
his eyes and made a silent comment.
"Enjoying yourself, Roswald, I see."
"I'm having a ball."
*"Don't be sad, it's you that gets all the
fun."*
"Just keep me in the loop."
"Understood."

CHAPTER nine

Loreto

Houston is a rich city but filled with motorists and long loops of interstate and intrastate highways. Loreto peered through his car windshield and squinted at the hot bright sun that loomed over him as he drove through

Highway 75. The towers of Houston's City proper came into view as he sped his BMW 528i towards the seat of Houston's government. He enjoyed this part of his job, but he didn't always feel that way until he realized that he was about to be in the middle of a great and momentous period of history. The words of Mr. Mercer rang in his memory - "Mr. Kennedy will be the mouse and we will catch the big white tiger." There were no tigers in Houston, not of the animal kind. But Loreto knew that the tiger might actually reside in this busy city. But then he knew too that the tiger, the Last One, might be in any of the cities that the other team members of F5 would find themselves in.

"Going in." The thought came to him not as a question but as a declarative sentence. Michael was keeping tabs on Loreto.

"Yes. I see the office building from here."

"Just be yourself."

"No, I won't need to do that. I've got my credentials. Howard Loreto, new press secretary to Governor Huntsman."

Loreto pulled into the car park and took a look around before getting out

of his car. He took out his sunglasses and put them in his pocket, and then removed his leather briefcase from the boot of the car. A jet formed a stream of white clouds in the sky above. He saluted it mentally and then walked towards the revolving doors of the Governor's office building.
He knew where to go and did not need to ask any questions. He had studied this place well. He knew who to approach and that person was a poker-faced receptionist typing diligently at her computer. She made him wait, although he had greeted her clearly. Loreto hummed a song in his

mind and looked intently at the woman. She had red hair, red lipstick and a red scarf over her loose-fitting buffalo check black and white tent dress.

Finally, she looked up and said, "May I help you?"

"I'm Howard Loreto. Reporting to Governor Huntsman as his press secretary."

Her manner changed, and she was transformed before his eyes. Her face was wreathed in a smile and she immediately stood up. "Oh, I am so glad to meet you, Mr. Loreto."

"Good to meet you too, Ms. - er-"

"Carbiner. But you can call me Greta."

"Greta." He repeated.

"Let me take you straight to Governor's office. His secretary's name is Ava Rossiter."

They made their way up the sweeping staircase that led to more offices and corridors on the upper floors. "I'd take you through the elevators, but they are being serviced at this time. And," she paused, looking over her shoulder at him. "The stairs are a pride and joy of the Governor's office. The building was constructed in the 1800's and the stairs were put in by hand by very talented artisan carpenters."

"I appreciate that, Greta." He did admire the very beautiful way the stairs flowed up and the marble steps with a massive oaken banister on both sides. "It reminds me of an opera house staircase."

"Funny you should mention that, Howard. The building used to be an Opera House. It was converted in the '60's when a new Opera House was constructed not far from here." She stepped onto the landing of the third floor and turned to the right. The office of the Governor was behind the closed mahogany doors. She tapped on the door and then pushed in without waiting for an answer. Greta led Loreto to the desk of a mature woman who wore her spectacles on the tip of her nose. She was fair and had cornflower blue eyes. When she saw Greta, she looked slightly disturbed and then smiled. "Sorry, Greta, I am very busy today."

"No worries. I've brought Mr. Howard Loreto - the new press secretary."

"Oh. Oh!" Ava Rossiter smiled at Loreto. She didn't shake his hand. "Well, I knew he was coming, didn't I? Ok, let me take a moment." She lifted the telephone and dialed a number. "Mr. Loreto is here, Governor." She looked at Loreto more closely as she listened to the voice on the other end. Ava gave Loreto a screening look and then suddenly hung up the phone. "Greta, why don't you take Mr. Loreto in?" "My pleasure." Greta's voice sounded silky and she led Loreto into the inner office of the Governor.

Huntsman was a tall and heavy-set man, with silver hair and long nose. He was standing by the windows rehearsing a speech. His voice was deep, and like many politicians, rich in tone. When the door opened, he turned and saw Greta. A smile touched his lips and then he became more serious when he saw Loreto. "Hello, Greta. I see you've brought my new press secretary. How are you, Loreto?" He shook hands with him.

"Good, Governor. I'm honored to be your press secretary."

"I'll leave you two alone, then." Greta said shyly and disappeared behind the door.

"Good timing, Loreto. I'm just now going over a speech that I will be delivering to the Chamber. I have not had this edited but if you like I'll ask

Ava to send you a copy. Have you already got your office and computer?"

"No, sir. I don't have any clue where they might be."

"Oh." He frowned. "Ava was supposed to have got you situated." He picked up his phone and dialed Ava. "Ava, why don't you drop what you're doing and take Mr. Loreto here to his office? And," Huntsman added with a more ominous tone, "give him a copy of my speech for the Chamber of Commerce."

Ava was looking even more perturbed when Loreto came out of the

Governor's office. "Let's see, I have forgotten myself." Ava said timorously.

"No need to worry. I am sure that you have a lot of work to do." She looked at him with a smile that told him she was becoming more sympathetic to him. "Oh, Mr. Loreto, I am in dire need of help. I seem to be getting too much work and there is only me. The one aide of the governor has resigned to marry and left the state. I think Greta would like the job, but she has also a lot of work to do."

Loreto felt a bit uncomfortable but then he was immediately reminded that this was part of his work - to listen and look. "No, I'm sure that is going to be ok soon. I think if you just told me where to go I can find my office."

Ava smiled again and leaned her hand on his arm. "No, I need to take a walk anyway. Here, I've got a copy of the speech." She took a sheaf of papers and gave them to him. "I will send you an electronic copy." Ava led him back out of the office and into the hallway where the air seemed much cooler. "It's right down this corridor." She was a thin woman, dressed very well in a designer suit, and her nails were painted brightly pink. "You have family with you or are you single, Mr. Loreto? Don't mind if I ask these questions. I like to pry."

Loreto smiled back and said, "I'm single. But I do have a girlfriend. She's going to be joining me in six months. She is working in Florida, but they can't let her leave due to the workload."

"Oh? Oh. How sad you're apart. Here's the office. The computer's all ready and the IT man should be by soon."

They parted in good terms and Loreto watched Ava walk back to her office.

"She's a sweet lady." Michael gave him a thought.

"Yes."

"I'd make her my best friend."

"She is a bit of a dear."

"Girlfriend? That's news."

"I want one, Michael."

"Sorry."

CHAPTER ten

The weather was pleasant enough when Jack Kennedy woke up that morning. His first glance at the expansive window in his master bedroom was that of a beautiful azure sky that seemed to descend up on him - bowing perhaps, to greet him. There were no clouds, and it reminded him of a great sailing day in Maine. He had memories of sailing with his siblings, on the Sound in Martha's Vineyard.

Jack stepped away from the window and sighed. There wasn't anything for him now, not really. He was whole, yes, but he didn't have the people he wanted in his life. Mercer gave him some hints that these people would join him someday. So many questions came to Jack Kennedy as he went about getting ready for the day. Michael texted him just then and asked him to meet him at the corner cafe by the Park. Jack wondered what it was going to be like, being a patsy. He was not used to being ordered about, except when he was in the Navy. That was leagues of time before now.

The doorman bowed as Jack approached. "Hello, Mr. Cruikshank. Good morning. Hope you have a great day!"

"Thanks, Pete." Jack smiled and then went through the doors. It was a crisp Fall day, and the breeze that ruffled his chestnut brown hair felt good and braced him. It was a nervous feeling that came to him though at that moment, and then he focused on getting to meet with Michael.

Michael sat with his hand around a heaping mug of coffee. Steam swirled out of the black liquid. Jack looked at Michael's face and read that Michael had no real agenda that morning. Just a friendly coffee meeting. "Hi Jack, how are you?" Michael greeted him and shook hands. Michael saw the anxious glance that Jack gave him before settling down on the chair across from him.

"Not bad. How are things with Michael?"

"Visiting - had to get some people straightened out. You know how the entertainment industry is like. It's a zoo, lots of excitement, they all need to be reined in, somehow."

"I can see there are scores of new shows in the rags. I'll be frank with you - I don't know a damn thing anymore about what is happening in the entertainment field. You know I'd be happy to help but what does a man like me do with all that?"

Michael smiled and bent him a level stare that reminded Jack of Mr. Mercer. "No problem. You're the writer that just made it big in Publishers' Weekly. Don't forget."

"Oh, that." Jack took the cue. "Well, it took me a while to write that - not sure if it would be a hit - "

"It is, and it will make you famous. You don't mind being famous, do you, Jack?"

"Oh, no." Jack paused as the waiter gave him a cup of coffee. "I'd like a brioche and a wedge of cheese, please"

"No problem." The waiter left them alone.

"I'm not nervous about being a famous writer." Jack said, warming to the topic. "I kind of like the idea. I know that it will be a break from all those months of being holed up in my office, typing out the novel."

"Do you need me to do anything for you at all before we go for the launch?"

"Yes, actually." Jack said with almost a shy smile. "Can you provide me with an escort? I'm not real good with being er- "

"No, you won't be mobbed. I don't think this time they will." Michael looked at Jack consideringly. "Are you uncomfortable for some reason with women liking you and wanting you to be friends?"

Jack waited to answer as the waiter came back with his order. "Well, I'm not into this sort of thing. I hate the attention. That's where my trouble is."

"Ok." Michael said, reading his words accurately. "We won't do this introduction to your book like throwing you to the wolves, as they say. No. The first book launch will be an hour of signing books. That will be with my secretary, Josephine. She and I are like this." He held his two fingers together. "If you ever feel the need to get away, then just tell her. I'll be nearby, but I'll have to let you handle this to see how you feel about being a new celebrity."

"Good. That's fine."

They ate in silence. While they did, a few of the women customers who came in gave Jack a second stare. Jack noticed them and ignored them. He felt as though a tug was at his heart. Michael looked at the women as they passed. "I'll have to make arrangements for your book tour, by the way. I'll send you via email the schedule."

"Good."

Jack still felt a bit wary of the attention. It was a new experience. The time in Heaven removed something of his humanity - perhaps that was good. The women who were throwing him glances were all modish, pretty women. But he didn't like to entertain them.

"Michael," Jack said suddenly. "I'm going to have to cut this short. I'd like to do some shopping, sight-seeing, all that jazz. Just let me know any updates, ok?

Michael stood up at the same time Jack did. "Ok." They nodded and then Jack left.

"My thought is that Jack Kennedy is not the same anymore."

"No, Mr. Mercer. He's not."

"We may have to help in some way."

"Perhaps Jack will have to get acclimated."

"No, this is more of a substantial change from the Jack Kennedy of history."

"We will see how he navigates."

"Yes. We won't want to have the women throw themselves at him. He is quite an attractive man as he always was."

"We have to find a way to have him make the news.   Celebrities.   That sort of thing."
"Indeed."

Michael peeled off a few bills and tossed it on the table before he left the cafe.   As soon as he got out of the door a cab came and he got into it. "Hello Joe, how are you?"   Michael said in a light manner.

"Mike, you gotta be careful."   Stan was a rotund man, who wore a Yankees cap.   His teeth gripped a cigar that was unlit.

"You telling ME to be careful?" Michael laughed.

"This place - I am not sure you want to - "

"Shut up, Joe.   Take me to my office."

"Ok, boss."

CHAPTER eleven

The bookstore was not crowded at 10
a.m. the next morning. There was a
good atmosphere in the store, people
were there browsing, some were
consulting the staff about the latest
publications, or enquiring about
books they wanted to find but needed
help finding. Jack came into the
store, clad in a conservative navy suit,
his hair slightly muffed by the breeze
which he characteristically brushed
back from his brow. There was no

real change to the atmosphere, but Jack felt a slight tightening of his nerve endings and he took a quick survey of the store. Nobody there that looked up when he arrived. Yet he could tell there was a small wavelet of some current that ran across the store.

A young woman, wearing a brown check jacket and pants, stepped forward to greet him. She was about 20-something, and her lapel displayed her name: Josephine Brand. Her smile was disarming as she said, "Mr. Cruikshank, I am Josephine Brand. Michael told me to look out for you here."

"Nice to meet you, Josephine." He looked past her head and noticed some people in the back lift their heads as they heard Josephine say his name.

"Let me take you to the author's corner. There's a pile of your books on the table, a Sharpie pen to sign with, and then a nice blow up picture of you and the book in the background."

Jack felt a sinking feeling. No, not a big poster picture of himself. Really no. "Is this poster necessary?"

"We need to make it a successful launch, Mr. Cruikshank." Josephine said without missing a beat.

"Looks like you are used to all this sort of thing." He noted.

"Well, I AM your publicist." Josephine smiled, this time with a hint of mischief.

"Let's go then!" He said stifling a sigh.

They went towards the back of the store and true to life, his likeness stood in a poster board next to the desk which he would sit in. He ignored the poster as much as possible and sat down. Jack Kennedy, as Mr. Jack Cruikshank, was becoming anxious and he didn't like it. Where was all the confidence when he was running for office? He didn't feel as though he could call up those feelings. There was a shuffling sound at his side and he looked up to see a dark haired, middle aged woman, sporting a Barnes and Noble identification card. She had a very pale face, with bright red lips, and a black blazer and checkered skirt. Her demeanor was of someone of authority. "Hello, Mr. Cruikshank, I'm Mildred Harpy. I am the manager of the store. So pleased to meet you, and to know the author of such a very interesting book. I feel as though you have so much wisdom, so much knowledge of history."

He smiled at her, rising to shake her hand. "I'm very flattered to hear that. I happen to have a History major, so it isn't really uncommon to know a lot of history." He added, "It's something a lot of readers should be looking into. You know that history will repeat itself?"'

"Yes, well..." She said vaguely. Her eyes glazed over and then she gave him the rote spiel of what he would be facing that morning when the store would be getting more customers.

"We've put a lot of your books on display at the window, and then some more pointers to have the customers find you here."

"Good!" Josephine interrupted. She clearly had a low opinion of Mrs. Harpy. "Why don't we settle in then, shall we? I am going to find you a cup of coffee and a bottle of water, Mr. Cruikshank, and then all you need to do is sit and let yourself be yourself. Would that work?"

"Great, thanks Josephine. I may call you Josephine?"

"Oh sure!" She sang out before she disappeared to find coffee and a bottle of water.

Mrs. Harpy stared hard at Josephine's retreating back before saying slowly, "We do not mind publicists, Mr. Cruikshank. We just hope that we don't have a melee when the people find you."

"Melee?" Jack repeated, trying to control his smile.

"Yes. You have a lot of people who might be interested in buying your book and we want the process to be orderly. Now," She leaned towards him, warming to her subject. "Just sign your name on the front page, and then direct them to the cash registers right over there." She waved a bony hand over the front of the store. "And please, don't hold up the line. They tend to be very chatty, especially about history or whatever they might be thinking about, and you might have to interrupt them - it's rather rude, I know, but really some people need to be reined in."

"I'll do my best." Jack said, picking up the Sharpie pen.

Mrs. Harpy looked up at him with a worried frown and then saw that he smiled. She sighed with relief. "Oh well. We do have to sell books, now, don't we?"

Jack said nothing, but he did flash his winning smile at her and then watched her leave with relief.

Michael dropped in an hour later to find that Jack Kennedy, alias,

Cruikshank, was indeed a very popular person in the store. Josephine met Michael at the front and told him of how popular Jack was and that the majority of the people who went to ask for his autograph were women, of a certain age, and even older ones who kept saying to each other that Jack Cruikshank reminded them of a famous person but that they couldn't figure out which one.

Michael smiled amusedly at this report. "Good. That's excellent. We are all eager to make sure Jack gets as much out of his debut book and generate interest in his upcoming works."

"Yes, of course." Josephine said with her hands clasped in front of her. Michael led them to where Jack was in deep discussion with a student of history, and then stood to survey the line that flowed from the desk where Jack sat. Indeed, the proportion of women to men was heavily in favor of the former, and Michael felt glad. He thought to Mr. Mercer, "This is coming along well."

"Good. What about any news people to take photographs?"

"Josephine thinks they are due anytime."

"Good. Jolly good."

As if on cue, a reporter from the New York Post happened to come by (as arranged by Josephine) and started to mill around the bookstore. Josephine signalled him to come over to see Jack and he nodded his head, following her lead. He didn't really linger much, but he did manage to capture some pictures in his unobtrusive digital camera, of Jack speaking to the attractive student and the long line of would-be readers and fans.

The reporter smiled at the sight and spoke to Josephine, "I'll have this in the morning edition. Watch for it, Josie."

"Thank you very much." She said with a formal voice.

"How about meeting me for a drink later?"

"Not sure about my schedule, Frank. I'll have some other people I need to shepherd through."

"You tell Mike I need him to update me with my new rates."

"No need to tell Mike." Michael appeared by their side and said to Frank, "I'll be very generous, that is for sure."

"Great!" The reporter sniggered and left.

"Why do we put up with that guy?" Josephine complained.

"We must be fair, Josephine. The Post is the best way to showcase new celebrities."

CHAPTER twelve

Lohar stepped off the curb and crossed the busy intersection to get to his office. He had been working for Judge Mandel for a couple of weeks and it was going smoothly enough. He avoided passing by Mrs. Krebs' desk, but she usually found a way to greet him, as she greeted everyone. "Busybody." He thought.

"Hello Mr. Lohar, did you enjoy

the weekend?" Mrs. Krebs asked smilingly.

"Yes, I went for a sail in Martha's Vineyard. How was your weekend?" Lohar replied knowing he had not gone for a sail but was instead keeping an eye on Jack Kennedy's activities.

"Oh, Martha's Vineyard. How cool!" She simpered. "I was with my grandkids. They all wanted to go to that chocolate factory restaurant on the Upper East side. Lots of calories, but we got a lot of walking done to counter that!"

He turned away and headed for his office. But, something on the counter of her desk made him detach himself from his physical self and look through it. Open on Mrs. Krebs' desk was a copy of Newsweek. Jack Kennedy (alias Cruikshank) was on the cover, his face smiling as he was captured on camera talking to an admiring fan. The title on the cover page was "A NEW HERO."

Lohar made a note of the magazine and then quickly ruffled over the pages to get a complete reading of the article on Jack Kennedy.

Lohar went to his office as usual, and closed the door. He opened his computer and then quickly reviewed what he learned. Jack (Kennedy)

Cruikshank was touted as a new hero, someone who was lauded for his book "History Recalled." The article spoke of Jack being a great intellect, trained in History, educated at Choate and then Harvard, and seemingly poised to become a big star not only in the literary world, but in the celebrity world. Lohar made a thumbs-up mentally. It was all going to be everywhere then - Jack was going places.

The door opened, and Judge Mandel came in. "Lohar, did you see the file on Senor Gilberto - the Avelina File?"

"No, sir. That's the file that

Rossiter was going to follow up. I'd ask him."

"I can't wait to find him. Why don't you see if his secretary has the file? I have a need to consult it."

"Would it not be on the V drive? All our files are housed in that - "

"No, I don't want to have to dig through it. Just go find it and then send it to me via email."

"Sure."

The Avelina File was something Lohar had no access to, at least, in the physical world. Rossiter was the guy on it and he respected his owning this file. Justice Mandel looked concerned and so it gave Lohar the idea that this file might be of interest to JFK's case.

Lohar logged into the V drive and identified the Avelina File. He knew that his accessing the file would log his information on the file - all files that were accessed or modified had an IT stamp on who accessed it and who modified it last, and would be there for IT people to see. Lohar ignored it and then removed his IT identity before he logged off. It was a nice perk for an angel to have and it made everything easily accessible to Heaven.

Lohar left the file in his computer

for a moment and decided that even if M asked for the file, that knowledge might not necessarily be enough to return his log in info into the V drive to keep everything kosher. Lohar asked Michael, "Michael I have this situation."

"Don't worry. I will have Judge M have no recollection of this request. It will be expunged as soon as he has read the file. We don't have to worry about it."

"What about the enemy's surveillance?"

"The enemy has been identified there and that person has asked for a leave of absence due to health issues."

"Good."

Lohar examined the Avelina File while he had the chance and then filed the case away in his mind. He sent the file to Justice M and closed the trail.

"What is in that file, Lohar?"

"It's about this man Ever Avelina, who lives in Mexico. He is a client of the firm. He owns land in both Texas and Mexico on the border. He is asking Madden to argue on his behalf to let him acquire land in Texas so that he can continue with his business dealings without the issue of torts. He is a real criminal, from what I've learned. Madden is not good."

"Any connections with Dallas yet?"

"Madden served in the circuit court in Dallas at the time of JFK's assassination."

"Then we want to have all we can find about Madden's connections when he was at Dallas. We want to find out about whether there's a money trail too. Let's see if we can access the financial files of the law office."

"I'll work on it."

"I'll also ask Loreto to see if there's any connection with Governor Huntsman."

"Oh, that will be helpful."

CHAPTER thirteen

The door to the dining room was closed which told the butler that Mr. Ellis was in a private conversation. Breakfast was getting cold but the butler, Mr. Vargas, would not dare to knock and upset Ellis. Piqued with curiosity, Vargas put his ear to the door and tried to figure out the conversation, even though it was one sided.

"Damn it, what is this about Jack Cruikshank?" The voice was thunderous.

"Well, I keep seeing this guy everywhere, in the dailies, the TV magazines, even the Wall Street Journal is asking him for his opinion. Why the hell is he talking about the time of the Cuban missile crisis? I can't stand that!"

Vargas tiptoed away and took his tray with him. The cook saw him come into the kitchen. "What, he doesn't like the eggs?" Mrs. Cole said with a snort.

"No, the boss is on the phone. He's not in a good mood."

"Well, I don't want to hear the complaining that he never got his breakfast."

"No, I'll not let you know what he said."

She looked at Vargas and then smiled slyly. "You are a gossip. Tell me!"

"He's up in arms about this famous writer. Some guy - what was the name? Something like Cook or something."

"Ellis is always suspicious of them writers."

"I guess."

Governor Huntsman found Ava filing her nails when he got out of his office. "Ahem." He coughed.

She looked up and slid the nail file under her notebook. "Yes, Governor?

"I'm going to be out for the rest of the day. Tell Loreto I have some of my releases on my desk. I can't bother to walk it to his office."

"Of course, Governor."

"I'll be at the golf course, and I'll be meeting some of the businessmen from Dallas there."

"Ok, boss."

He left without another word, and bumped into Loreto who was just coming in the door. Loreto smiled quickly, "Hello, Governor. How are you?"

Loreto received no reply. It was as though Huntsman did not see him at all. Loreto checked himself and saw that he was actually in his physical form and then shrugged.

"I'm sorry, Governor H is going out for a golf round with some business people. He likes to do that once in a while." Ava said apologetically.

"Ok, fine. I wonder whether you know where the releases are for this week?"

"Yes, they're over on his desk. He said you are free to take them."
Loreto counted his lucky stars and went inside the governor's office.
He found the releases on the desk but then saw that there was a file on Jack Cruikshank underneath. Loreto made a small note of the file's contents and then took the releases with him.
"Interesting discovery." Michael's thoughts came to him.
"Yes. JFK's getting the attention of this guy."
"So where has he gone off to?"
"Golfing. Business buddies."
"Let's send our spirits over to the golf course."

"Over and out."

"Look, I'm not that worried, Huntsman," the man in the Burberry cap said to the governor as he started to address his ball. "There's no way anyone can be that stupid. This Cruikshank author, where did he come out of? Have you anything on him?"
"Nah - well, yeah. Gummy, we need to get our thoughts together on this. This guy looks really like a close relative of the President. JFK! I got

my chills seeing him on the cover of the Newsweek magazine."

"You are seeing things, Huntsman." Gummy Bellows snorted. He stopped a bit while Huntsman swung at his ball. The ball flew a little short and stopped right before the bunker on the 3rd hole.

"Damn." Huntsman said dully. "I guess I am seeing things. I can't get over it. I had this thought that this guy was JFK come back to life."

"No way. That is not true. The video shows it. Everybody - the whole damn world saw it on video. On tape, then, if it's been that long ago. Do you have anything on this guy Cruikshank?"

"Preliminary PI work says he is a bachelor, comes from New England - somewhere in Maine, I think. Then that he went to school in Santa Barbara and took his Master's and PhD in Government and History at Harvard. He lives in Manhattan in a real nice place by the Park. I've asked a few people to tail him. I think he's not seeing anyone at this time."

"Any past affairs?"

"If there were any, we don't have that info. He does have a way with the girls, if the Newsweek rag can be trusted. And I don't trust it much."

Gummy took his turn to address his ball. He and Huntsman said little and then Gummy's ball took off and flew high, sailing way over the bunker and landing to a rolling stop a few feet from the hole. Gummy gave a satisfied grin at Huntsman and they both took themselves off to the golf cart.

"Nice weather - guess we are a lucky couple of golfers."

"Listen, I need to ask you to put out the word that this Cruikshank might be a relative of JFK. These days I'm wary about those who want to find some way to look into stuff. Did you know that Cruikshank's book is called

History Recalled?"

"Aw, that's just your nerves,

Huntsman. That guy ain't anyone.

You just sit tight. Tell nobody.

You'll be fine."

CHAPTER fourteen

It was annoying to Roswald, who had never had to work for a living in his angelic life, that he had to cut the grass at the Ramona V estate in the rain. Yet that was what he was doing. Rain came down, creating puddles and dampening him from head to foot as he stood on the edge of the lawn mower, that mower that was intended to cut green blades of grass in the rain, or in the sunshine.

"Enjoying yourself, Roswald?"

"Michael, you try it - it's a lot of fun."

"I'll take your word for it." Michael *went on to say, "You know that this woman who owns this estate - she's real interested in Jack now that she's seen him on The View."*

"Oh really?"

"She wants to go to his celebrity party that we're throwing for him here in Beverly Hills."

"And can I be of any help?"

"You need to be close by when she tries to win a little one on one with the President."

"Will do."

"Good. Let's plan on you talking to the housekeeper and finding some more things about Mrs. Atwell's connections. Maybe hang around to see if Mrs. Atwell wants to throw JFK a party."

"Can you ask God to stop the rain? I'm soaking wet."

"Sorry, it's not allowed. He's got a wish to wash a few bad spirits away."

Roswald lifted his eyes upwards, his lashes wet with rain water. Then he hung his head and went on with his work.

"I'm here. What is it that's so important?"

"The Cruikshank guy. He looks like a dead ringer for that dead President."

"I am sure there are plenty of them around. He's not particularly outstanding in the looks. There's so many All-American faces in this country. Why this guy?"

"Did you see his new book, *History Recalled*? He's trying to challenge the high points of history - from World War I, the Second War, Vietnam,

Korea, and then the assassination of JFK. It's eerie. What kind of mind does this guy have to think these events are all related somehow?"

There was a pause. "Ok, so maybe he has an enlightened mind. What's his background?"

"Not a lot. Ivy league schools, working as a writer. We don't have much on him."

"Look for any friends or family. He can't have been spawned out of nothing."

"I need some cash flow. I have to --"

"You'll get it. Just expect a few credits in a week or two.

"Thanks. I appreciate it." Then he added, 'What if we find somebody in his circle of friends?"
"We just do what we do well."

CHAPTER fifteen

The Pacific Coast highway was smooth under the expert hands of Michael who drove his fast Porsche down the wide and winding roads. The sun was setting low over the horizon. His face was inscrutable as the conversation in his car settled to a few humdrum words. "I'm guessing we will be fashionably late." Said Jack Kennedy next to him.

"Yes. You really need to make an entrance."

"Is Josephine going to be there?"

"No. Another of the F5 will be there. You might recognize her but if you don't she will be acting as someone who wants to be part of my business but isn't quite ready yet. She's a freshman at UCSB. So she will likely be there as an observer while serving canapes."

"Oh ok."

"She will be your shadow, Mr. President. For the sake of our future meetings, I'll have to call you Jack.

You don't know what people are up to with their listening gadgets."

"I agree. You can call me Jack as before. I won't mind."

"That's good."

"So this party - is it all the book people in Los Angeles?"

"Yes. Big literary people. A few people who like to dabble in history. PhDs and so on. You will be in your element."

JFK laughed without much humor.

"I'm sure."

"I will bc mingling around too, so you'll have a bit of freedom to mix. I'll be there, Helena will be there, and a couple other of the F5 will be there.

So don't be nervous. Just milk it. We
will send over Helena when things get
too dicey - you'll know."
"Once she comes, what?"
"We will say our good nights. The
cameras will be clicking, and it will
be in all the tabloids and the
publishing rags. It will be what will
make everyone take notice."
"Have we gotten a few bites?"
"Some. But nothing definite."
"Who looks after you?" JFK asked,
and then realized who he was
addressing. "Sorry, I didn't remember
you were who you are."
"No problem. I'm your Man. I'll be
keeping you out of trouble."

Still, JFK felt a niggling thought. "I get the oddest feeling that there's more badness in store for those who are helping me. Am I wrong?"

"No." Michael said abruptly.

JFK felt the caution in Michael's voice. So this was more than being cat and mouse, he thought. This was the good versus the bad in real action. It made JFK feel suddenly alone - even though Michael assured him he would be protected.

As if reading his mind, Michael said kindly, "No need to fret, Jack. You really don't need to. Leave everything to the F5 Team."

The evening was cold outside the walls of the Abbey. There was a moon that shone intermittently as dark clouds scudded past it. Adelred stood up from his kneeling position after his night prayers were said. There was a thin sound of a passing vehicle outside way down below the side of the Abbey where the roads crossed in front of the grounds of the Abbey. It was not yet midnight, but Adelred went to bed and kept his watch next to his pillow so that he could get up for vesper prayers at 3 a.m.

He had not drifted that deeply into sleep when he sensed a presence in his cell. Adelred knew it wasn't Michael and he knew it was a malevolent presence. Adelred kept still and pretended to be asleep.

The door was not open, which made it clear that the Presence was spirit not human. There was a rustling sound, of papers being rifled. Papers and mail and books on the desk where Adelred would sit and go through his correspondence and read his holy books.

The Presence seemed to be looking for something. It was almost impossible for Adelred to keep still.

He wanted to leap out of the bed and confront it. But something kept him from doing so. "Be still." Michael's thoughts were almost imperceptible. There was a slight pause in the silence, and then the sound of the squealing of little animals that came to Adelred's ears. He wondered about that and then realized the Presence expressed consternation. He, this presence, did not find what he was looking for. There was a whiff of sulfur and then the presence was gone.

Adelred waited a few minutes and then sat up. *"You ok?"* Michael thought to him.

"Yes."

"You recognize the ghost?"

"No but I smelled sulfur."

"That's the Devil."

"I figured that."

"He's looking for something."

"He won't find it."

"If this happens again, you need to tell me and I'll bail you out."

"No, this is telling me we are getting close."

"Yes. That is true."

"Fine. You will be under my special watch."

"Thanks Michael."

CHAPTER sixteen

Jack Cruikshank stood by the door
with a glass of scotch in his hand. On
his left stood a tall blonde who wore a
very revealing outfit that Jack tried to
shield from his sight by staring out of
focus. He wondered where Michael
had got to.
The party was in full swing, with
plenty of people from the literary

world. There were people in very different types of garb, a few individuals in outlandish clothes, which he figured were the celebrities that liked to wear the newest fashions from Paris and New York. Several of the guests were prone to burst into gales of laughter, which Jack wondered was genuine. Did these people really feel that happy or were they just aware of the significance of this event out of all events in their lives? Jack decided no, they weren't really happy. They were all slightly out of whack, he opined to himself. The blonde drifted away to his relief and then was replaced by another woman who clutched his arm and told him she really needed a crash course in English history. Jack tried to extricate himself from her but it seemed fruitless.

"More appetizers, Mr. Cruikshank?" A voice spoke on his other side, the unoccupied side, and Jack looked down at the owner of the voice. He saw it was Helena, and was glad to see her.

"Yes, please. Tell me, will they ever bring us some real food?"

"This is the only food they will serve, I am so sorry to say." Helena said with a sympathetic smile. "I think that what happens usually is that everyone decides it's time to go home and they find another place to eat food."

"Ok."

The woman who was at his other side twitched her lips in impatience.

"Listen, Jack. May I call you Jack? I want to ask you what your inspiration was to write your book."

Helena again smiled sadly and left them. She passed by Michael who stood by and they exchanged glances.

"He's needing some help." Helena said to him in her thoughts.

"No worries. We are all waiting for some other guests to arrive."

"That's what I'm afraid of."

"Never fear, Helena."

The guests did trickle in again after a lull. One guest that entered the room was a woman in her sixties accompanied by the professor who had encountered Helena. The couple stood hesitantly at the edge of the room and then focused at Jack. They spoke in an undertone and then they broke off of each other's company. The man went in search of a drink while the woman sidled over to JFK's side. The woman who had captured JFK was summarily dismissed by the elder woman who smiled falsely at him. "I'm so very glad to meet you, Mr. Cruikshank."

"Please call me Jack."

"Oh, Jack. Thank you! My name is Angelina Porter, I teach over at the university."

"Which one?"

"Santa Barbara. I'm in the Political Science department." She said with a titter. "It's so awesome how your career has dramatically risen in such a short time. What is the reason for this, I wonder? I have read your book, now, and well, I can imagine why. But I wanted to ask you in your own words...?"

Grateful for a more intelligent conversation, and pleased that she thought so well of his work, JFK replied, "I'm lucky I guess. I am a history buff, and always was. I am sure that because I love history, I get a second sight into what might have been the undercurrents throughout the European historical landscape."

"Ohhh!" Mrs. Porter said with a sigh. She rolled her eyes and then as she did so, the man who came in with her approached. "Hi, Oliver, I'd like you to meet Jack Cruikshank. He's a wonderful conversationalist as well as an historian and author."

The man named William extended his hand and bowed slightly. "Pleased to meet you. I teach in the same

university - but I'm in the English department. Oliver Steele."
"Oh I see. I happen to enjoy literature myself..." Jack bent slightly towards him and they went into a deep discussion of William Blake whom Jack had thought of with admiration. Helena watched Jack and the professor named Oliver Steele with skepticism and then communicated to Michael the meeting. Michael gave an assent that this was what he was waiting for. She turned to go to the back where she removed her apron and headed out of the door. Her job was still on but it had changed at that moment.

Michael approached the trio talking
amongst themselves and patted Jack
on the shoulder. "Well, I see you've
met a few people, Jack."
The professors from UCSB looked at
Michael with impatience. They were
unhappy at the sight of another person
to interfere with their interview of
JFK.
"May I introduce my literary agent,
Michael Stevens?" JFK said to the
couple. "Without his expertise, I
would still be struggling writer."
The couple's expressions did not
change. "I see. Well, that's nice."
Mrs. Porter smiled slightly. "Perhaps,
Jack, we can talk again. Maybe you

would like to come visit UCSB and give a talk?"

"That would be nice. Thank you." She gave him her card and then steered her escort away.

"They don't like you, Michael." Jack said.

"Were they too onerous?"

"Intense. I don't know what I've done - they were like a laser beam on me."

"Yes. I am sure they were." Michael spoke lightly, belying the harsh expression in his face.

"I'd be glad to find some food for us, but I don't have any idea where we could find it."

"Famished?"

"I don't like these little finger foods."

"No, I guess they're not great."

"Should we leave?"

"I'm afraid we have to stay a bit longer. You're the guest and as such, you should stay."

"To tell you the truth, I am bored." JFK said coolly.

"Just a few more minutes." Michael glanced at his watch. "Helena is just now finishing her shift. The food brigade will be over soon. Let's just mingle and find as many more fish to fry."

JFK nodded and wandered away, his glass in his hand and in need of replenishing.

CHAPTER seventeen

Helena stepped out into the darkness without much hesitation. The air was cool, and there seemed to be a haze where the city lights shone. The LA traffic that roared a distance away gave her no qualms. But she checked her surroundings just in case. What she next heard was an angry exchange.

"I don't know why you made him an invitation to the college! Why did you do that? You know that would have been something the committee would have had to vote on!"

"I wanted him to come and that just came out of nowhere. I am so very sorry." A woman's voice was calm and pleading.

"Well, I hate to think that people would have to review the man's credentials and just because he wrote ONE book, he is now a *cause celebré*."

"Max, I am so sorry I even dared to ask him to our little soiree. He won't remember. I will not expect he will remember."

"You had better damn well hope he won't remember."

Their voices lowered after that and Helena didn't catch the rest. Instead of walking to her car, Helena stayed and tried to figure out where the voices were coming from. She saw Oliver Steele and Mrs. Porter getting into their car.

"Did you hear anything?" Michael's thought came to her.

"Couple arguing," she replied. *"They seemed to be unhappy that the woman invited Jack to a party."*

"Was it the man Steele?"

"Yes it was."

"Good. We need to make sure Jack makes that party."

Helena read the smile in his tone.

"Going off line." His thoughts drifted away.

CHAPTER eighteen

One sunny day when Roswald was working on the bougainvilleas, a low-slung automobile swung through the opened gates. He glanced at the car and knew it was a Ferrari, black in color, with darkened windows. His interest piqued, Roswald slid out of view and watched its progress to the main house where it stopped. A moment later, the driver side door opened and a man emerged. Roswald looked at the man and realized it was someone who was recently in the news. *"Michael, I've got a sighting,"* he thought.

"Who?"

Roswald's gaze scanned the figure that stood by the front door.

"Secretary Vincennes. Oscar Vincennes."

"Interesting. Why would he want to visit your employer?"

"I'd like to know that myself. Going in to listen and watch."

Roswald became invisible and followed the Secretary of State Oscar Vincennes into the house.

"I'll let her know you're waiting in the library, Mr. Vincennes," Mrs. Danforth was saying as they entered the house and walked through the hallway.

"Good. Tell her to take her time." Secretary Vincennes said with a drawl. He was tall, slender, walked with a cane, and had a patrician bearing. There were several generations of Vincennes that went backwards to the French revolution. Vincennes was in his 60's, yet did not show it.

Roswald, invisible, kept himself apart from Vincennes. Roswald perched himself up on the bookshelf by the window when Vincennes entered the library. He seemed to be familiar with the place for he headed straight towards the French windows and closed them. He waited for his hostess by sitting on the divan, one leg crossed over another.

The door opened. "Hello Oscar. What a delightful surprise." The hostess, clad in a long midi dress of a grey hue, came inside and went to his side. She was an attractive woman, a brunette with blue eyes. Ramona

Atwell let Vincennes kiss her on the cheek then on the other.

"I need your help, frankly my dear Ramona," He started saying.

"Something is rattling my bones and I need information."

"What is it?" She asked, settling herself down on the opposite chair. She had a mildly interested look.

"I've not heard that you were even in California. Is everything alright?"

"No, not everything. In fact, I'm sure that I'm in a heap of trouble. I can't stand it. That feeling that I'm being watched."

"Oh, but you are, dear Oscar!" She went into a peal of laughter. "You are, after all, the Secretary of State." "No, not like that, Ramona. It's different. I can't place where it started. Maybe it was in a news bulletin. Or maybe when I was watching the television. But," he paused. "This makes me feel as though one of the people in my family has done something terrible." Ramona looked at him intently. "And how do I figure in this? I am not familiar with your ancestors nor any of your family - except your dear wife, Annie."

"No, not her - not anyone here where I am - but somebody in my family. A dead ancestor."

"Oh." Ramona spoke in a soft tone. There was a small pause. "You need to tell me everything. What about this feeling. Is it something about the latest news where you went to Taiwan? Or is it anything to do with that dead relative and Taiwan? What?"

"No, no. Not foreign affairs…" He trailed off. "Maybe. I wanted you to help me. You're the best hypnotist in the USA. Can you help?"

She stood up, closed the curtains and went to the desk behind him. She pulled out a pocket watch and then went to his side.

"Ok. I'll have to do this this way. Sometimes it is easier to focus on an object while one is being led into one's subconscious."

Ramona Atwell took the object from her desk drawer and then went to his side on the divan. He looked at the pocket watch with some distaste but said nothing. She began by holding the pocket watch before him and let it swing slightly. To and fro. To and fro. "You will feel relaxed, Oscar. Feel the weight ease out of your body. Yes. Lean back and breathe in and out with leisure."

Oscar's eye lids began to close slightly into slits. His hand loosened its grip on his cane.

"Tell me what you want to unburden."

"Someone. Someone dead." His lips were moving unbidden. "I saw him the other day."

"Who?"

Oscar said nothing.

"Is it still you, Oscar?"

After a pause, he said, "No. It's Gregory."

"Gregory. Who are you, Gregory?"

"Never mind that. You need to tell someone. He's come back."

"Who's come back?"

"The President."

Ramona's breathing became shallow, quick. "The President." Her voice was calm. "The one we have now?"

"No. No. No." Oscar's head moved as if he was in the grip of a restless thought. "He's come back. He died and now he's back. It's terrible. We can't see why he's back. No. No. No."

"Let's try to be calm, shall we, Gregory?"

"You don't understand. You don't understand. We made damn sure. We were assured he would die. We saw it on the telly."

"You are speaking of whom?"

"Jack."

After a moment, Oscar stirred and sat up. The ghost of Gregory had left his body.

Roswald, who was observing this, left the room and sat far above on a tree top. He didn't think. But he was with Michael. Both sat together unseen. A shadow left the house. It floated, aimless, almost without knowing where it would go. A moment later, the shadow was accosted by a white cloud that was low on the ground. Roswald and Michael watched as the shadow was led away. The sun had been behind the clouds but that same moment it came out and brightened the area. The heavy atmosphere was gone.

"Well, we now know that this Gregory was in on the conspiracy." Michael said.

"Someone is now taking Gregory away. For interrogation." It wasn't a question. Roswald looked thoughtful.

"We'll make sure that Oscar has 24/7 surveillance."

"That would be good." Michael looked up and then disappeared from sight.

When Oscar Vincennes came to his car, Roswald was still working on the hedge a few hundred feet away.

CHAPTER nineteen

The grounds of the abbey that afternoon were sparsely populated. Adelred stepped out into the sunshine and relished the soft breeze. The grass was cut earlier that day and the smell of green cut grass was like a happy thought in his senses. He walked to the small grotto close to the chapel and sat down on a stone bench. He pulled out his breviary and leafed through it and found his marker. He was about to say his Evening Prayers and made the sign of the cross.

A shadow fell across him and he looked up. He couldn't tell who it was for the figure obliterated the sun and looked darker than it would have. "Sorry, who is it?" Adelred asked, squinting. He realized it was the monk who was in his room the other night.

"It's Brother Marcus." The dark figure moved and Adelred saw it was actually Marcus. A slight odor of sulfur came to his nostrils. Marcus made a move to sit next to him. He was smiling, looking harmless. His teeth were crooked, Adelred noticed. "I wanted to ask you whether you have made any decisions about your staying here permanently?"

"No, not really." Adelred said in response. "Are you in need of my cell? I noticed the Abbey is chock full of postulants."

"Oh, no no. Nothing like that." Marcus said, his eyes merry. "I'm just being officious. That's my job. I have to make the rounds and ask about the visiting friars. You said that you were en route to the San Bernardino area?"

"Yes. I was asked by my superior in New York to stop here for a couple of weeks. I didn't realize you were the person in charge of visitors. Abbot Jonas said nothing of you being like that. I had no idea."

"Oh, perfectly alright." Marcus said. "I see. So when are you leaving us?"

"Next Sunday." Adelred replied. He folded his breviary and stood up. "Sorry, I need to go back to my cell. I forgot my devotional."

"Perfectly alright." Marcus stood up as well. "See you at supper."

"Yes."

"By the way, do you have family in New York then, or is that not where you are originally from?"

"I'm from Piscataway," answered Adelred. A severe pain started on the base of his neck. "See you later then."

Marcus watched him walk away and a frown descended on his face. He looked angry by the time Adelred had disappeared inside the abbey. Adelred sought the confines of his cell and once he was inside, went to the window and stood looking out. He saw nothing now. He was not in the right position to observe the grotto.

He massaged his nape and after a bit, the pain stopped.

"Adelred, what happened?" Michael asked. His thoughts were faint, almost imperceptible.

"Marcus tried to kill me."

"I know - that son of a bitch."

"I'm fine now."

"He should be avoided at all costs."

"I can take care of myself."

"Well, I don't think you should put yourself in further peril. That so-called monk is capable of making you sick."

"I thought - well, I thought I was immune."

"You have a humanity that is prey to pain and suffering," Michael reminded him.

"That is quite apparent." He replied ruefully.

"Now, sit down and relax. Do as you were going to do."

"I take it I can't go around and make my rounds tonight?"

"I think we need to be cautious."

"You know I can leave at any time."

"That might have to be the case."

"You really think this man is going to be a problem?"

"No he won't. You'll be ok. You need to stay here until your time is up."

"Ok."

CHAPTER twenty

The following morning, Adelred joined the others at the chapel and took his usual place as the opening hymn began. The chorus of male voices was impressive. Adelred glanced over at the place where Marcus would have been standing.

But the place was empty. Adelred returned his attention to his breviary and joined the others voices with his.

Breakfast was served as usual at 7:30 a.m. At the hall, the monks filed inside to take their places at the wooden benches. At each table, where the monks sat, were bowls of oatmeal and a glass of juice. A piece of handmade bread was also perched next to their bowls. A rounded spoon lay nestled on top of a brown linen napkin.

"Let's begin." Spoke the Abbot who stood at the end of the table. "Bless us O Lord…" He intoned. Then he motioned all to begin eating after making the Sign of the Cross. "It's a beautiful day, isn't it, fellow brothers?" He asked cheerfully as he tucked into his bowl of oatmeal.

"Yes, it is." Several replied.

"I want to make an announcement, actually." The Abbot said. "Brother Marcus has been taken to hospital. He happened to have fallen into the ditch where some workmen had left tools. I'm afraid he banged his head pretty badly. The medical men tell me that he will need to undergo surgery to repair the gash."

"Oh my!" Spoke a timid-looking monk. "It's really too bad that the workmen left their things - it's going to be on us to be responsible for their carelessness."

"I'm afraid that is true," Abbot nodded.

"How long before he returns to the Abbey?" Asked another monk.

"That is going to be up to how he recuperates." Abbot said, sounding

less interested in the topic. He moved
on with another subject altogether and
the other monks went along with
more interest.

Adelred kept to his thoughts and
slowly consumed his oatmeal. A
slight glimmer of light shone at him
from the window and he glanced up,
squinting. Then he went back to his
oatmeal and then finished his juice
before asking to leave for his day's
tasks.

Two days later, at the last meal of the
day, Abbot came in late and sat down
looking perturbed. He said grace on

his own, then stabbed his meager portion of calf liver and ate. Adelred and the other monks could not help but notice his behavior and they all sat waiting for the coming outburst.

It did not take long.

With a loud cough, Abbot stood up and took the lectern where the reader of the bible would usually stand to read out the day's chapter. "My dear brothers in Christ, I have some bad news."

All of the monks sat like stone, expectant of bad and dire news.

Abbot's face was flushed. He seemed uncomfortable. It seemed as though he had seen a ghost. Adelred clutched his rosary and felt a bit dizzy.

"I have to announce that Brother Marcus became worse from his head injuries and now he has died. His brain developed sepsis and they could not save him. Let us say a silent prayer for our Brother Marcus."

All of the monks bowed their heads except for Adelred. He felt flushed with gratitude. It was all he could do to stand and cheer. But a thought from Michael gave him the nudge to bow his head finally and look sad.

CHAPTER twenty-one

Lohar sat staring at the computer screen in front of him and became aware that the drive that he had found was not something everyone in the office knew about. His instinct was to keep his thoughts undercover as he went through the motions of deriving the files within the drive. He found

one cryptic file named Avel_Bk_1962
which was actually not accessible as
it was an old file that nobody had ever
seemed to review. At least, the last
time it was accessed was in 1975.
Lohar made a few fast-strategical
moves to keep the file looking
untouched but he copied it to his
desktop where he opened it.
The file was about Ever Avelina, a
horse breeder in Austin, TX.
Michael's thoughts descended upon
Lohar and said, *"This is interesting,
eh, Lohar?"*
"Yes," replied Lohar. *"Looks as
though this cattle rancher and horse
breeder has, at sometimes*

communicated to Mandel - something that makes no real sense. Mandel doesn't really deal with that sort of client nowadays."

"Even more interesting to delve into."

"I think we need to find out why Avelina had to ask Mandel to handle his corporate account. Old school friends, perhaps?"

"Avelina is no longer able to give information. I sense that he is now in a nursing facility in Texas. His son, Ever, Jr. Is working the business."

"Anything to do with JFK?"

"I don't see it."

"Only that Avelina had his bank in Dallas. Wait," he felt excitement course through his veins. *"I see that Avelina's banker at the time was Governor Huntsman's father, George."*

"Curiouser…"

"I am sure that Huntsman is not alive now."

"His son is. Loreto works with him."

"I don't see much else. Just a lot of transfers of rights to George Huntsman's estate."

"That is a huge clue, Lohar, if I may say so myself."

"Going to have to find out if there's also a money trail. Yes! Here's

another file that has records of transfers of millions of dollars to George Huntsman's bank. But - it's from different accounts."

"I'll talk to Loreto and see what he can dig up."

Michael's Spirit left him and Lohar felt a slight chill. He heard a door close outside and the voice of Myron Biggs, Mandel's right hand man, speak to one of the staff. Lohar logged off the computer and turned to the paperwork on his desk.

Biggs came in without knocking.

"Lohar? What about the latest report on our case against Mrs. Cartwright's estate?"

Lohar looked blandly at him.

"Working on it. The judge decided not to hold court today. Something wrong with the electrical circuitry or something."

"Electrical circuitry?" Biggs leaned over his desk. He had huge broad shoulders, a shock of curly dark almost black hair, and pig like features. "Hell, that's not an original reason to call off court!"

"Sorry, that's all I know. I will be making a report on the case after it reconvencs next Monday."

Biggs sneered at him. "You look real cool and collected, Lohar. You should know that I'm onto you."

"Sorry?"

"Yeah, you hick from Ohio. I can sweep the floor with you. I wanted Mandel to pass on you. Sick of ignoramuses. First year associates at that!"

Lohar leaned back and met his furious stare. "I don't know why you're mad, Biggs. I know my place. So why don't you just tell Mandel that I'm incompetent? I don't need to work for the likes of you."

Biggs looked taken aback at the calm and cool reply. "You need this job!"

"No, I don't." Lohar said quietly. "I think YOU need to cool off. Whoever she was isn't worth it."

Lohar got up and passed him on the way out of the office. Biggs sputtered and then stared at his retreating back with his mouth agape.

CHAPTER twenty-two

Lohar still felt a sting from his confrontation with Biggs. He walked leisurely out of the law office and down the hall where the elevators were located. After he got out of the building, he expelled a sigh of relief and sought a distant eatery to take his lunch. He sat without paying attention to his surroundings. He was deep in thought. The waitress had to ask him twice what he was having. Lohar looked up at her and saw her smirking at him. "Sorry, had a little problem to think about."

"Suits me fine, Mister. You can think all you want, but I need to tell the cook what he should give you for your lunch." Her Brooklyn accent was thick and Lohar appreciated it. He was tired of the officiousness of lawyers that he had met in his short career on earth.

"Ok, what about a Reuben sandwich, no mayo, and some French fries?"

He asked. "Oh, and a nice cold beer,
please."

"What kinda beer?"

"Oh, ah - *Dos Equis*, please."

"Good choice. I'll be back.
Meantime, you forget that shit that the
office give ya." She smiled at him
with a wink and then ambled towards
the back.

Lohar smiled at her too and then
wondered what Biggs was up to.
He closed his eyes and then he saw in
his mind's eye that Biggs was sitting
at his desk. Lohar pursed his lips.
"Don't worry, " Michael's thought
was comfortable to sense.

"Yeah. I am going to be needing some body armor I think."

"It will be there." Michael reassured. *"But you won't need it."*

"Thanks, Michael." Lohar's fears were allayed.

Biggs sat at his own desk and took his cellphone out. He looked up at the door and made sure it was shut. He punched a telephone number, then held the phone to his ear, and waited.

"I want to talk to Ever, please."

"Si, it is Ever. Who is calling?"

"Ever, this is Myron Biggs. Of Mandel Law."

"*Madre de Dios*, why are you calling me now?"

"I apologize but I needed to ask you whether you had asked anyone here to work on you file. As you know, your file was closed. Did you need any further help? If you do, you should ask for me. I am Myron Biggs, Mandel's Chief of Staff."

"Puñeta. That was a long time ago. I cannot believe this. I want to - no, I demand to know why my file is opened. Is that what you are saying, that it is opened?"

Biggs started to feel sweat at his nape. Hell. He was in a pot of shit. "Look, Ever, I am sorry. I think that I made you worry for no reason. I am sure that this was just a big error. Somebody got into it and didn't know what for."

A torrent of Spanish came at him from the other end of the telephone. "Hell with you, Mandel Law. You will be hearing from me!"

"No, please, I wanted to ask if there was - "

"NO! Not at all. I want my file destroyed. You do that for me. I want it destroyed." The voice became high pitched, almost pleading.

"I can't destroy files, Ever."

"Biggs, you need to keep that file closed."

The line went dead and Biggs sat
back flabbergasted. His face was
dark with rage. His focus was now on
Lohar. It made no sense. But then he
needed to investigate this problem.
He was thinking fast. Then he got up
and went to Mandel's office.
Mandel was at his desk but he was on
the phone. When he saw Biggs, he
motioned for him to leave. It was a
confidential call.
Biggs was about to leave but
something on the desk of Mandel
caught his eye. The New York Post
was opened on a page and the picture
of Jack Cruikshank was on the page.
The headline said: "Up and coming

author Cruikshank to speak at UCSB - is he the new local hero of the Big Apple?"

Biggs straightened up like a shot and then fled the office. He became almost frantic in his reaction that the secretary and receptionist both commented that his departure was like he was on fire.

"Biggs, my dear Karen," spoke Mrs. Krebs, "is not well. I've noticed how he is always terrorizing everyone. And getting alarmed at everyone's mistakes. He's not well." Mrs. Krebs looked at the open door with some trepidation.

CHAPTER twenty-three

Ava looked in her compact mirror to check her lipstick. Having come back from lunch, she made sure that her makeup was as fresh as it was when she first applied it that morning. She was making a large O of her mouth and dabbed at her lower lip when the door of Huntsman's office slammed shut. She jumped up in her chair with surprise and then she sighed.

"Oh, that man!" She said severely to no one in particular. "He is going to be the death of me one day."

"Who's going to be the death of you?" Loreto asked as he walked in the room. He was bearing a small bouquet of flowers.

"Oh, the governor, Mr. Loreto." She said with a slight laugh. The flowers caught her attention. "Oh! How pretty!"

"I was asked by the florist to give it to someone who might need it. The person it was meant for had gone on vacation."

"And is that now mine?" Ava asked with a big smile.

"Yes, actually. It's yours. I'm just the messenger." Loreto said with a slight bow.

"Thank you, Mr. Loreto." She accepted the flowers and got up out of her chair. "Let me find a vase. If the Governor comes out and asks for me, tell him where I've gone to."

"Sure thing."

She disappeared with the flowers and Loreto idly stood by her desk. He tuned up his aural abilities and tried to know whether the Governor was in his office. He was in luck. Huntsman was on the telephone with someone.

"Ever, calm down." Huntsman said in a pleading tone to the person on the other line. "This is all a big mistake. It's all closed. Nobody will ever find out."

"I hope not, Governor. If it ever did, there will be the devil to pay!" Huntsman squirmed in his seat. "Ok, ok. What is the reason they said they had to open the file?"

"Not really said. No, the man, Biggs, that is his name. *Madre de Dios*, I have to take a pill I am still shaking. No really, Governor. It will come out. It will."

"No, that will never happen. We have it on good authority that anyone who dares to open this case will be destroyed."

"Oh? And that will make everything alright? Listen, that file was supposed to be destroyed years ago - after the murder. If it gets revealed - *Madre de Dios* - this will be our problem and we will be facing a long, long time in prison for all kinds of crimes."

Huntsman squirmed in his chair. "I will tell Biggs to destroy it and find out who got into the file."

"I want this done, Governor. Otherwise there will be reporters and lawyer and -"

"No," Huntsman said firmly. "No." Avelina rang off and Huntsman sat back, sweat pouring down his face. He leaned forward again and spoke into the intercom. "Ava, I am taking off the rest of the day." There was no answer. He slammed his hand down on the table with great force.

Ava came back with the flowers in a vase of water. She found no sign of Loreto in the reception area of the office and sighed. "What a nice day it has become!" She murmured and then lovingly set the vase of flowers on a corner of her desk.

At the same moment, the door to Huntsman's office flew open and the Governor came through looking pale and sweating. "I need to take the rest of the day off, Ava. I feel like it's this hot hot weather."

"Alright, Governor. I will reschedule any appointments, then?"

"Yes." He paused. "Yes. Do that." He looked a bit lost and then left the office.

CHAPTER twenty-four

Lohar knew that his days in Mandel's office were numbered. He ran down the back stairs of the building and out the door where the dark night enveloped him. His thoughts went to Michael. "I'm going to be getting some action, Michael."

"I'll back you up."

"Biggs is on the rampage. He's found out from someone that the Avelina File was opened."

"Did he trace it to you?"

"Not exactly. I had a pseudonym that I used."

"Good." From Michael's view, he could see Lohar walking fast along Third Avenue. "Don't go underground, Lohar. That will not work."

"Agreed."

"Huntsman was the main connection for this file."

"Yes. The file was about JFK's assassination. We need to see why Mandel has possession of it."

"Got it."

"Did you see who ordered the kill?"

"Someone out in California." Lohar paused as he went into a side alley where he levitated high up onto the top of the building. "I feel a heat coming."

"I see Biggs. He's on your tail."

"Damn. I think there will be a lot of fireworks coming."

"Do your best. I'll be watching." Lohar's appearance changed as he became his natural angelic self. He wore a grey loose tunic and pants, and his shoes morphed into suede leather boots that had wings on their heels. He surveyed the streets below and

saw Biggs barreling down, his head
down as though he were tracking
someone.

Suddenly, Biggs looked up and saw
Lohar hovering above him. "YOU!"
Biggs exploded in anger. He shook
his fist at Lohar. "I'm going to get
you, asshole!"

"Not at all." Lohar flew a quarter of a
mile from where he was. He landed
on top of the next building.

Biggs roared and then shot up from
his position to approximately the
same height where Lohar was located.
Biggs' appearance became sinister,
and his face became dark, lean and
wore a black goatee. His hair, curly

before became a skullcap and horns
came out from either side of his head.
A large sword of fire came out of
nowhere and Biggs caught it.
Lohar smiled mockingly at Biggs.
"Come and play, you devil you."
Biggs lunged up at Lohar but Lohar
was quicker. The flaming sword
swung at Lohar and barely missed
him.
Michael watched them and kept
himself from intervening, although
his instincts told him that Biggs was a
huge demon.
"Look behind you, Biggs."
Biggs glanced behind him and then
Lohar leveled a spear tipped with

gold at Biggs and threw it at his chest. Biggs staggered back and stumbled on his rear end against the blowing heater beneath him, the spear lodged in his chest. The spear became wrapped in a glowing flame and spread from Biggs' chest down the rest of his body. Biggs uttered a loud cry, which echoed all over the skies. "Well done, Lohar." Michael said approvingly.
The figure of Biggs had burned into a small cinder that glowed momentarily, until it ebbed into a dark and hard piece of coal.

CHAPTER twenty-five

The next day was busy for Lohar. He felt relief at arriving at the office and knowing that Biggs was no more. But he did not expect the lack of news about Biggs's demise. *"No, that's because they aren't sure where he is. Remember Biggs became a piece of coal."* Michael informed him, reading his thoughts.

"Got it." Lohar said with a slight nod. He entered his office and immediately smelled sulfur. *"Ok, he's been here."*

"Let's get it decontaminated."

"I've got just the thing to accomplish it."

Lohar set his briefcase aside and from his pocket removed a flask. He also put on a pair of *pince-nez* to survey the office. From behind the lenses of his *pince- nez* he spied the dark spots where Biggs' fingers had touched the surfaces - the desk, Lohar's computer, and the doorknob. Once the spots

were identified and decontaminated,
Lohar put the flask and pince nez
away and began to start working.
There was a knock on his door.
"Come in."
Justice Mandel entered and looked at
Lohar with a pained expression.
"You need to come to my office."
Lohar got up and followed him out
the door. Mandel said nothing until
they arrived at his office.
Mandel's office was large, and took
up a great deal of real estate. The
room was dark paneled in rich
mahogany, and there were rows of
legal bound books, statues of past US

presidents and even a bust of Marcus Aurelius.

His desk was massive, and on top were different piles of folders. Some were folders that had been there for a long time since their sides had curled up slightly and became yellow. Lohar decided that Mandel was not as impressive as he looked, but that was only because Mandel looked like a cowering lion instead of his usual intimidating stature.

"I'm afraid we don't know what happened to Terry Biggs." Mandel said right off the bat. "I am in the process of advertising for a replacement if he doesn't come in by the end of the week."

"Sorry to hear that, Judge." Lohar said coolly. "He could be late today, or tied up with a personal problem."

"It's after ten a.m. Biggs is usually here before everyone else. No. I think something's gone wrong with Biggs." He leveled a stare at Lohar, whose face looked as bland as possible.

"If that's the case, how can I be of help, Judge?"

"I need you to take over his cases - get that one he's been working on - his secretary knows it."

"Understood."

"And then I want you to help Mrs. Krebs in screening applicants for Biggs' job. I don't want to take you away from your cases, Lohar. I think that's all." Mandel turned away and sat down. His face was impassive but his hands shook as he took a pen to write with.

Lohar left Mandel and headed back to his office. *Michael, I'm sure you heard.* His thoughts flew to his captain.

"Yes. Don't work on that guy's case. Let them simmer. You can ask his secretary to have the cases electronically sent to you. Don't touch the man's things."

"Understood."

"I'll send some people to apply for Biggs' job. You will have some company but they won't be required to talk to you this way."

"That's a relief."

"Good work, by the way."

"Thanks."

CHAPTER twenty-six

Adelred was feeling more relaxed for the first time since he arrived at the Abbey. This morning he was able to attend Morning Prayer and share the breakfast meal without having the feeling and knowledge that the evil monk Marcus was giving him. No difficulty in his physical well-being, no real feelings of anxiety - and mercifully God seemed to be smiling down at him today.

This confidence that God was approving his existence and work was confirmed when, as he made his way back to his cell, the Abbot confronted him with alacrity.

"Greetings, Brother Adelred!" Spoke the Abbot, his florid face looking at him from his great height. "How are you doing these days? We have you for another week or two perhaps?"

"I am supposed to leave at the end of the week, Abbot."

"Well, I have to prevail upon you dear Adelred," said the Abbot. He took him aside and lowered his voice. "Since Brother Marcus has shuffled off his mortal coil, as it were," he chuckled softly. "We have a need for someone to take his place in our administrative department. Our donations have been coming in and nobody's had the chance to make heads or tails of it. You DO have a head for figures and numbers, do you not?"

Adelred had an inkling that this might be what he was supposed to be doing. A small star above him shone in the stead of Michael who was listening. "Why, I do, actually. I have a degree in Math. Not an accounting degree, though. I think you could use someone with an accounting degree, don't you?"

"Heavens, a Math degree!" Exclaimed the Abbot. "That will do!" He took Adelred's arm more tightly in his hold and dragged him further into the shadows of the hallway. "Now, let's get us to the admin department. Brother Keller will make you comfortable with all the nuances of getting things all straightened out. Brother Marcus did the actual deposits and that will mean you have to use the Abbey's Prius to get around to the bank. You can drive, can't you?

"I can." Adelred's nape was becoming more and more heated with excitement as he half-followed and half- hung on to the Abbot's arm to the department where he would spend his remaining days in the Abbey.

Abbot gave him the run of the office, and with Brother Keller, a slightly stooped elderly man who merely gave him the login and password of their only computer, Adelred was in. The presence of Brother Keller did not faze Adelred, but he was extremely sensitive to anything that might be interpreted as working for the enemy - which was preposterous because,

Adelred reasoned, he was working for God's Team.

Later that evening, Adelred sat in his cell, feeling worn out, his head full of numbers and calculations, and sorely wishing he had the comfort of his prayer book in his hands. At the moment, he was suffering from a headache and it would not go away.

"Adelred, I hear you have replaced the evil Marcus?"

"Yes, dear Michael. I have."

"Congratulations!"

"Yes thank you." Adelred replied in a failing voice. They were, as always, in thought together. Yet each one could recognize the other's thought because they had a unique voice.

"You look tired. Let me ask what else is wrong tonight?"

"I have a beast of a headache."

"Ok," Michael paused. *"That is the energy from Marcus. He may be deader than a doornail but his energy still exists."*

"That is bad."

"Bad indeed," Michael said thoughtfully. *"Why don't you look up at the crucifix on the wall and stare there while I talk to God about this headache of yours. It won't be but a moment."*

Adelred looked up at the crucifix and stared at it. Unbidden, a prayer came to his mind and he went along with it. He sighed a small, short exhalation of a prayer and then, the headache left him.

Michael said, *"It's gone, right?"*

"Yes. That is good. My fervent thanks."

"Now, I want you to make some investigation into the donations. Find out who has been giving large donations and from what state of the country. I want the names and addresses if possible. I can send you Helena to help get the data and she will make it all presentable to me."

"Is that all I should do?"

"For the time being, yes. I must say good night. God rest in You, dear Adelred."

The invisible star that shone at Adelred faded and the room fell into gloom. Only his small fireplace glowed with dying embers. Adelred hobbled out to his cot and slid into his blanket making himself warm under it. His eyes drooped and then he soon fell asleep.

CHAPTER twenty-seven

The day at the Abbey was very quiet and orderly. The monk that Adelred worked with was a simple man, and gave him as much support and help as he needed. Adelred went through the spreadsheet and started to enter all the donations that arrived the day before and found that there were a great number of them that were rather large - in the thousands of dollars, from people who seemed to be elderly and hoping that the monks could pray for their intentions. One lady, from New York, sent a donation of $5000 and asked for the prayers for her husband's terminal cancer to be healed.

Adelred found himself saddened and yet made an effort to distance himself from these poor rich people who felt they could get their intentions to be prayed over and the money to sustain the Abbey.

The Abbey was not in a great deal of disrepair, he thought musingly. He sighed and went on with the rest of the list.

A thought of Michael arrived in his mind and Adelred was asked if he was alone. *No,* he replied. *The other brother monk is with me.*

"Don't worry, he's a very spiritually good soul. He will be given a density of thought so he can't be at all able to listen to our talking this way," Michael replied. *"Have you started on the donation spreadsheet?"*

"Yes."

"What do you gather from it so far on this first day?"

"A lot of donations, totaling sixty thousand dollars."

"I think that's a bit extraordinary, don't you?"

"Yes, I suppose so. I don't know how these places can get so much in one day."

"I would check to see where the most donations come from. Then, I would find out - let's see how much of the donations get to where they are supposed to go and then find out whether the abbey has a list of banks that they shelter their money."

"That's going to take a lot of work."

"Adelred, you are a very smart angel. Let's say we need this information in two days?"

Adelred sighed and then smiled with a sweet expression at his computer monitor. *"I also want to, Adelred,"* Michael added, *"make sure that this computer does not have anything in it that makes your investigations subject to monitoring by the Abbot."*

"Ah!" Adelred smiled as though he had been told something he already knew. *"I already made that assessment. Clean as a whistle."*

"Good. I don't like that Marcus getting his hands on the money that's

meant for good works and the upkeep of the Abbey."

"I will be done in two days, God willing."

"It is fine. I will send Helena for the information as I have some other affairs to tend to."

"How is our friend Jack doing?"

"He is good. Not to worry. Don't think about it much, alright? We have him in hand."

Adelred felt Michael's presence recede and then the room became more of a dull hue and Adelred bent his attention to the task at hand.

CHAPTER twenty-eight

Santa Barbara was a beautiful city that was always a joy to behold to anyone who visited for the first time. The trees were tall, stately and graceful as they lined the winding driveways and roads. A lush green carpet of grass made for a picture of rolling hills, and the stately houses and mansions that dotted the countryside were all so picturesque. The view from the helicopter ride where Michael and Jack Cruikshank rode hovered over the city. The lights of the evening began to flicker and soon a gloom became obvious as the evening glow from the horizon became more distant.

"Time we got here." Michael said with a grimness that Jack found concerning. Michael was at the controls of the helicopter. He seemed to know all that was needed in navigating a helicopter.

Jack nodded. "Yes, it's gotten a bit dark. Can we find where we are supposed to land?"

"I'll land us at the airport nearby. Then we will take my car to the reception. I have the address. The Steele couple are making this a big deal and the society pages are definitely abuzz about your appearance."

"Good. I mean, good that you can maneuver different types of motor vehicles and air - and maybe even sea?" He raised an amused eyebrow. "Being a part of Team F5 is fascinating, and this is certainly very exciting."

"I have trained with the best, and they have given me good marks."

"I can imagine. Michael I am so impressed."

"Let's not get too much ahead of ourselves, dear Jack. We are going to be in for a ride tonight. I want you to keep your eye on either me or Helena. She's coming to the party again as a server. She will pretend not to know you nor me but when we are there, you should mix and get to know a few people. Maybe strike up a conversation with some of the women there who are raring to get some private time with you."

Jack was taken aback and felt disturbed. "Ok, I know that I am the snare but I don't like going with women who might want to get me in trouble."

"Jack, your job is to get into trouble and we have to find out who it is that's behind that trouble, remember?"

"Women too, huh?"

"Yes, I'm afraid so." Michael's view of the airport came on their horizon. He spoke to the air traffic controllers and made arrangements to land.

"Guess this will be a party to end all parties," Jack laughed.

"I think it might be."

"Ok. I gotta talk to God and pray this will be something I can handle. It's been a long time since I ever got into a great number of possible bad guys and girls."

"You are prepared and you should be fine. If trouble occurs, it is possible that they will just want you to visit them for a private discussion.
"

"You mean, they might kidnap me?" The idea had lurked in Jack's mind but he had brushed it off.

"They might."

"Hell." Jack said in a hushed voice. "Michael, I will be frank with you. I've been shot at and plunged into the high seas and I've had my share of women, but this is making me nervous as all hell. I wish I could have packed a gun, or - "

"No, not a gun. You need to be totally in character mode. Just be what you portrayed yourself as Jack Cruikshank, elegant and erudite, and well-versed in the ways of the world."

Jack sat back and ignored the gathering view of the airport that Michael steered them to land in. His thoughts were all over the placc. Then he felt a certain peace and it made him remember the time when he was in the Second World War, when he was struggling to keep his PT109 boat afloat. He fought to keep it at arms-length or closer, then. But his prayers were that he would not die yet then. He became suddenly at peace in the middle of the warlike weather and the turbulent seas. It was a bit like being cocooned where nothing or no one would touch him and make him give in to his fears. Jack wondered about that later and now that he was about to make it through to another crisis that would render his last enemy powerless, it was almost like he was tasting the victory before he had it.

Jack remembered Mr. Mercer's words. "You have already died. You are no longer subject to death." He sighed and looked out the window. They had landed.

Michael got out and Jack too, got out into the tarmac. Their ties and jackets flapped in the swirling wind that the helicopter blades made. They ducked and ran towards the airport. They were with the mindless mass of people and made their way to the front where their limousine waited. Professor Steele and his wife, Mabel Porter, were at the door of their estate and cheerfully welcome both Michael and Jack. The Steele couple, as Jack thought of them, were very happy to see him again. Jack nodded his approval at their plush surroundings. There were a crowd of guests in the foyer where there stood in intervals high tables where drinks and hors d'oeuvres were served, and servers in tails went through the guests asking politely if they wanted more. The foyer stretch across to the end of the first floor, and on either side were large rooms, opened to anyone who would care to go inside for a brief moment of privacy. Some were there but most were there at the foyer to size up Jack Cruikshank.

Jack was taken by Mabel Porter's hand and she led him down the foyer and introduced him to all the hoi polloi of Santa Barbara. Each guest looked vaguely familiar and then Jack remembered them when they were still his contemporaries but they were so very elderly yet looked like they have drunk the waters of youth. Michael trailed him as he sampled the drinks and the enormous hors' d'ouvre's and listened as Jack spoke to his new acquaintances. It was obvious that the party was made to show Jack as a JFK clone to his former enemies and friends. Jack Kennedy made a lot of friends in his career and several dozen attended, some looking well preserved, some looking quite miserable and showed it.

Michael spotted Helena serving a few yards away and sent her a thought that reached her almost immediately.

"What do we know?" Asked Michael.

"All are his old friends and lovers and acquaintances - they all want to see if this Jack Cruikshank is actually JFK."

"Why did they think that? Someone's been talking." Michael answered with a chuckle.

"I'm nervous, Michael. I am worried we are the only ones here on Jack's side."

"I know. We have to let things go the way the plan goes."

"I'm leaving to be an observer - an unseen one."

"Go to it."

Jack stood next to a trio of interested guests and found himself wishing he had a bodyguard. His skin crawled as he passed a few of these people. He sipped his scotch, he hated winc, and then let the liquid slide with a fiery effect down his gullet. Michael seemed to be hidden from view and

Jack wondered whether he was purposely letting Jack be lionized to the fullest effect.

"Mr. Cruikshank," A woman came to his side and linked her fingers with his. "I want to ask you whether you could do an interview with the LOK show next Friday? I don't know if you have a schedule but I would so very love to interview you."

"Sorry, but I didn't get your name, sweetheart." Jack said, letting his hand still be laced with hers.

"Oh, I'm Jinny. Jinny Owlek, from NBC. LOK stands for Land of Knowledge. It's a show I do every month. Tell me you'd come." Her face was oval and had dark hair framing it. She looked oddly like someone he knew in his past life. His blood ran cold at the recollection. It was a struggle to keep his voice light and his smile on.

"I'll have to check with Michael Hanes, he's my publicist."

"Oh of course." Jinny smiled falsely. "Why don't I give you my card?" She slipped a linen card into his pocket and patted his chest. "I would love to have a nice dinner with you afterwards."

Jack was making thoughts seeking Michael. *Where on earth was he?*

He turned away from Jinny Owlek
and sought refuge in one of the rooms
where he drained his glass and felt a
cold sweat form on his nape. It was
awful, how that woman was the
personification of one of the women
he knew intimately.
Michael strode towards the room
where Jack disappeared into. But
when he got there, Jack Cruikshank
was gone. Michael looked around,
then went back out onto the foyer.
Jack had been taken out to another
part of the house, he surmised.
He looked for the Steele couple and
saw nothing of them. All the guests
had filed into the dining room.

Perhaps, Michael thought, that Jack was also in the dining room.

He thought a question to Helena. *"I can't find him."*

"He's not in the dining room. I checked. He was sending out an SOS."

"Damn."

"I think he's gone, Michael."

"Ok. Let's find him."

Michael turned on his heel and went to the door where he disappeared out into the darkness.

Helena and Michael joined up at the gate and slipped into Helena's waiting car. The limousine had disappeared and Helena's car became their only means to find Jack. "Look," Helena said, her eyes spotting a pair of tail lights ahead. "It's one of the cars from the party."

"Jack, can you hear me?"

"Loud and clear."

"Where are you?"

"In a car - blindfolded. I'm also in handcuffs and my feet are tied up. They caught me going into one of the rooms. Damn it."

"No don't worry. We're right behind you."

"Ok. I'm going to relax now. I have no other choice. This is something I

never learned when I was real. I mean, I couldn't let God take care of things. Hell, this is a bloody adventure."

"Relax. Keep talking to us if you want."

Helena spoke. *"No, I think that there are some people who can read our thoughts."*

"Let them." Michael scoffed. *"F5 is looking at all of these people and they are taking names and identification numbers."*

"Good."

Jinny Owlek lay sprawled on the couch of her host's home and smiled brilliantly up at Oliver Steele. "It's JFK. I can tell."

"How?"

"He just has that certain something." She grinned and kissed her fingers as if she were relishing the experience. "I think he felt something too but he wanted to repress it."

"Oh, Jinny." Steele said shaking his head. "It's a coup. We have the rehabilitated John Kennedy, thirty fifth president of the US, in our possession. We could get billions for him."

Mrs. Steele looked on the pair. "I'm sure we will but we could be getting into a trap."

"Mr. Ellis doesn't seem to think so."

"What does he know? He's been a recluse forever."

"I guess we just have to keep at him and ask him for the pay off."

"I think we have a few people to inform."

"What ever for?" Mrs Steele's eyebrows lifted.

"They will know." Steele said in a sober tone.

"I can't wait." Jinny giggled. "The fun times we had."

"You gotta be kidding. JFK isn't going to bed you again. You are a devil and a hag. If he saw what you really looked like - "

Jinny jumped up and flew at him in a rage.

"Stop!" Mrs. Steele shouted.

"I want you to die!" Jinny screamed.

Steele stepped back with fear in his eyes.

"Look, you are who and what you are. We are all awful. I can't believe all those who came back from their graves to see JFK in the flesh."

"I am sure they are having fun now. They are exulting that the JFK they knew and wanted dead is alive and for whatever reason, he is back."

"Did it ever occur to you both that JFK is back because of one reason?" Steele smiled with a sinister glint in his eye.

The other women sat silent and stared. "Oh. What would that be?"

CHAPTER twenty-nine

The skies were overcast in Houston
when Loreto ambled into his office
that Monday morning. He received
word that Jack Cruikshank was
kidnapped - news from his F5 team.
He felt a surge of energy in his spirits
and decided it was a good time to

visit the Governor's office just around break time when Ava would go off to have her morning doughnut.

He knew Huntsman was in his office. Loreto entered the outer office where Ava had her desk, a sheaf of paperwork in his hands ostensibly to tell Huntsman that his speech for the Holster Club at the Capitol Hotel was finished and ready for his review. As predicted, Ava was gone and nobody was guarding the governor's office. At least, nobody that Loreto could say. He looked at the door of the inner office - it was shut.

After standing for a moment, Loreto decided to knock on Huntsman's door before shoving it open. "Who the hell is that?" Thundered Huntsman, his face stormy as he looked at Loreto over his shoulder. Huntsman was hunkered down over a file cabinet, his hand in an open drawer.

"Sorry, Governor. Here's your speech for today's Holster Club meeting."

The governor's frown cleared a moment and he replied, "Ok. Leave it on my desk will ya? I'm busy this morning. I thought Ava would keep people out."

"She's busy somewhere, I guess."

"Damn that woman." Huntsman said under his breath.

Loreto laid the papers on the desk and left without a word. Unbeknownst to Governor Huntsman, a small receiver that was the size of a staple sat stuck under the last page of the document. Loreto wanted to keep track of Huntsman, and this was perfect for that task.

As Loreto left for his office, he heard the phone ring. Ava was still out. Loreto came back inside and without answering the phone, lifted the receiver and switched the phone call to Huntsman's desk phone.

Huntsman sat down to take the call and then he became stiff like stone as he listened. "Hell, what are you saying?" He murmured in awe.

"I've got the man Cruikshank."

"What happened?"

"Don't ask. I have to grill him later. He was at the party that the Steele's organized last night. I got him, Huntsman. We've got him." The voice was exultant.

"What do you propose you do with the man? Are you sure he's JFK?"

"I'm pretty damn sure. Jinny Owlek said so. So did the others who we dredged up from the depths of hell - they all attest he's JFK come back to life."

Huntsman showed little joy in his face. "What - ok, I don't want to know. You do what you want. I won't do any more for you, Ellis. I'm done. I can't handle this. Why would JFK want to come back? Is this another trick that your satanic friends are playing?"

Ellis laughed. "No, I think JFK wanted revenge. But I'm sure that the super will say it is HIS revenge. He really, really wants JFK and his stuff to die in front of his eyes. He told me so last night."

"Ok, I gotta hang up. You stop calling me do you hear me?"

Huntsman banged the phone down

and then sat back with his head flung back on the chair back. He made no movement. His mind was awhirl.

"Mr. Loreto told me you were looking for me?" Ava chimed in as she stood in front of him. She looked at him with mild curiosity.

"I'm fine. I forgot you were gone to get coffee."

"Ok. I have someone else on the phone. It's Justice Mandel. Do you want to talk to him?"

"NO!"

"Ok, don't shout at me. I'll tell him you're busy. Can he call you later?"

"NO." He stood up and paced the room. "Ava, do NOT allow any phone calls today. I have to concentrate on a project I'm working on."

"Ok. I guess you won't be seeing anyone then." She left the office and shut the door.

CHAPTER thirty

The morning dawn crept slowly over the Santa Barbara hills. The valley below the Bellingham mansion slept soundly - nobody had any inkling that the resurrected president of the United States of America John Fitzgerald Kennedy, sat alone in the basement dungeon of the estate. Nobody knew but a couple of angels stood atop the roof of the mansion, looking down at the valley as they spoke in low murmurs.

Helena and Michael were clad in their military outfits. Both were not exactly sitting on the roof but suspended in air above it by a foot.

"Roswald said he saw Jack getting tossed in the car. I am glad Roswald was on the lookout." Michael said coolly.

"What do we do now, Michael?" Helena asked, trying not to think of the dark figure that owned the very roof they sat on. "Shouldn't we go to a nearby tree top? This place is creepy."

"No. You're with me. I am going to get JFK to a safe place. But he needs to find something out for me first."

"I see."

"Roswald, are you with JFK now?" The thought arrived to them both:

"Check."

"Go through the house in your unseen mode and see who lives here. If you meet some evil force, you can let us know. We will be on standby."

"Check."

"Roswald," Michael surmised aloud, "would assure Jack Kennedy by his presence. It was going to be close and yet I fell there is something missing."

"We don't have evidence yet that this owner ordered the actual hit on JFK," Helena said.

"No. But we don't have to wait for the evidence."

"We plan to kill this Ellis, then,"

"There is a plan to do that, yes. But we need to see what else the others have found."

"Ok."

CHAPTER thirty-one

Jack Kennedy, alias Jack Cruikshank, sat calmly on a chair by the bed where he refused to sleep. His prison was a dank smelling, fetid place where rats ran all over and the world was somewhere off in a different planet. His only consolation was the presence of his allies, Helena and

Michael, and now Roswald, who appeared through a small window and stood in front of him the night before.

"Roswald here. You look all in, Mr. President."

"I feel all in. Thanks for dropping by."

"What can I do for you besides getting you out of here?"

"I could use a shower or maybe a glass of water."

Roswald handed him a long tall drink of water from nowhere.

"Thanks," Jack Kennedy smiled slightly and drank it all. He felt so much better and handed him the empty glass.

"The others are somewhere around. I wouldn't be too upset at this place. The rats are all clean and don't have rabies. I've made sure. There's a space closer to the window where you might be able to catch a whiff of air that's pure."

"Thank you again. May I ask how long you and Michael propose to leave me here?"

Roswald paused. "I'm afraid I am not privy to this information. But," he walked a bit further towards the door as if listening for signs of visitors. "I will be with you to keep you from feeling alone and getting depressed."

Jack Kennedy smiled gratefully.

"That is what I am beginning to feel. I can't stand this. It's worse than being in the Pacific Ocean with sharks trailing around."

"That's what they want you to think. You're in Santa Barbara, where the sun shines all the time. I have to leave you for now, but I will return."

"Ok."

Roswald left and the gloom came back to cloak the room. Jack Kennedy decided to sit on the bed and stretch his legs.

He leaned back and felt a comfortable ease that enveloped him. He closed his eyes and then opened them again, as if afraid that closing them might make him die and go into a pit of hell. Then he remembered who gave him back his life. He remembered why he was alive again. He needed sustenance. He slumbered and dreamed of eating at his favorite restaurant in Boston. He didn't know they were still around. He saw the old gang there, making jokes and talking all at the same time. He seemed to be at home.

END OF PART ONE

* 9 7 8 0 5 7 8 4 1 5 6 8 0 *